MiMi'S GARDEN

iT'S A KiD THiNG!

A GUIDE FOR BEGINNING GARDENERS

Written and Illustrated by

Maria Rock

Text and Illustrations Reviewed by

Alicia Rock

Hi! My name is MiMi. This is my dog Maggie. She follows me everywhere I go. We love to work and play in MiMi'S GARDEN on our family ranch. Everyone always asks me, "How did you learn so much about gardening?" I tell them my mom and dad own Andersen's Feed and Seed, a plant nursery. We all work together in our nursery learning about flowers, vegetables and all kinds of plants that grow around the world.

We love to read garden books, magazines and garden news. My favorite newspaper column is America's Royal Gardener. Every week someone special gets to be the Royal Gardener of the week. Maybe someday I will be the Royal Gardener!

Maggie and I love to garden-dream and share the joys of MiMi's GARDEN with everyone. I can hardly wait because it's gardening time again. We make our garden dreams come true with the help of all my garden friends in MiMi'S GARDEN.

Garden Vocabulary

Here are some new garden words for you to learn.

Definitions

AMENDING: covering moist soil with compost; turning the compost back into the soil about the depth of the shovel blade. This loosens and enriches the soil for planting.

CASTINGS: sand passed by a worm after it eats compost. The castings are filled with nutrients for plants.

COMPOST: a mixture of dead leaves, manure and things that decay.

GERMINATE: when seeds or bulbs first begin to grow roots and sprout new leaves.

ROOTBALL: where roots cluster, usually at the base of a seedling or a plant.

SEEDLING: a new plant that germinates from a seed.

SOW: when a seed is first planted.

THIN: to remove seedlings or plants growing too close to each other.

TRANSPLANT: to move a plant from one place to another.

Maggie says don't forget BONE: a treat for your dog!

Can you name all the tools for MiMi'S GARDEN? When you use the proper tools in the garden it makes the job so much easier. If you don't have lots of garden tools you can borrow them from a garden friend. Sometimes we need three shovels and two rakes for a garden job. Our neighbor Sam has lots of garden tools. He shares them to help us in our garden.

My friend Mo and I spend the morning getting the garden ready for planting.
Cleaning up the weeds in MiMi'S GARDEN is an important job. My mom says
to keep after weeds when they are little because when they grow big they are
hard to pull. Maggie likes to pull weeds, too. Oskadis (say: oh • ska • deese), our
Icelandic filly, likes to eat them up! Thor, Mo's cat, is our local weed inspector.
Good job garden gang!

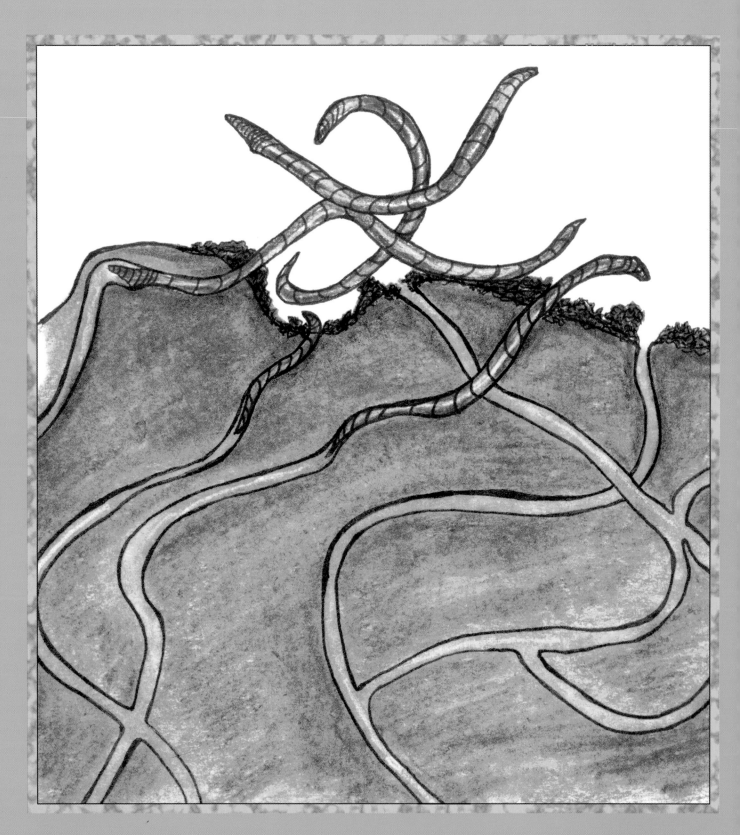

Worms are Mother Nature's little helpers. They like to eat the compost they find in the soil. Worms dig tunnels to look for food which helps the soil to breathe. Roots will grow easily in this loose garden soil. Worm tunnels make good trails for water to travel deep into the soil. Worm castings also enrich the garden soil. My dad says if you find worms in your soil it's a good place to plant a garden!

We are amending the soil in MiMi'S GARDEN. Maggie likes to watch as I turn the soil over twice to loosen the soil and mix it with compost. We are always happy to find lots of worms. Hanna, our hen, loves to eat them! Most of our garden worms wiggle back to safety under the soil. Maggie would you like to share a worm with Hanna? How about a chocolate-covered "worm"?

Seed Packets

1. Name of plant

2. Tells what the plant looks like, what you can use it for in your home and garden, and how long it lives.

3. What kind of soil makes the plant happy. Where to plant it. How deep to plant seeds so they pop up. How to make fine soil. When it blooms.

4. Thin: means to remove extra seedlings. If they grow too close they will not do as well in the garden.

5. How to get an early bloom. Care of the plant.

6. Weather conditions to watch for before planting.

7. What a seedling looks like so you don't mistake it for a weed and pull it out!

Note: Seed packet information can vary, but they all give the correct growing information. Questions? Ask your local nursery person.

Cosmos
Sensation Mix

Burgundy, cyclamen and pastel pink symmetrical daisy-like flowers. Poor soils are acceptable for these hardy flowers. Great for borders. Makes great flower bouquets, lasting longer if water changed daily. Grows to 5 ft. high. Annual.

Growth Tips: sow in well-drained soil. sun-lovers, protect from strong winds. Cover seeds with 1/4" of fine soil. Use a strainer to make soil fine. Flowers mid-summer to autumn in warm climates.

Thin: to 12" to 15" apart when seedlings are 1". Transplant thinned seedlings with ease in another part of the garden. Germinates in a few days.

Garden Tips: for early blooms start seeds indoors around 8 weeks before the last spring frost. Easy keeper.

When to Plant in Your Garden: sow after last heavy frost.

Seedlings look like this:

Now that we have pulled out all those weeds and amended the soil we can plant in MiMi'S GARDEN. All the plants in this book can be purchased as seeds or plants already growing in containers. Let's learn how to read the back of a seed packet before we go shopping for seeds. Sometimes we need an older garden friend to help us read our seed packets. They can learn new things about their garden with us! Look for MiMi'S GARDEN seed packets that are easy to read for gardeners of all ages.

My friend Rosa and I love to go garden shopping together. Today, we are at my family's garden shop. We are going to bring all sorts of things home for our garden. We take turns riding in the garden wagons and have a great time. My dad lets Rosa and me pick out all kinds of fun things to plant in our garden. Most of our garden seeds are annuals, which means we have to replant them every year. Do you like to shop for your garden supplies?

When Rosa, Maggie and I got home Mo was sowing some tomato seeds in our mini-greenhouse. We are really excited to see that some of the lemon cucumber seeds are now seedlings! Some of our seedlings are big enough to transplant into MiMi'S GARDEN. Today we are planting a bunch of our seedlings that we grew in our mini-greenhouse. Would you like to have a mini-greenhouse? They are easy to make with the help from an older garden friend.

We all like to take turns planting seedlings in MiMi'S GARDEN. Rosa is very gentle as she plants our lemon cucumber seedlings. We all know that it's important to water our new plants, seedlings and seeds. Just like us they all need a drink! Mo always wants to use the waterwand. He likes to water everything in his path. Hey Rosa, did you ask Mo for a drink? Ready or not here he comes! Watch out Maggie! Do you enjoy watering your garden and your garden friends with a waterwand?

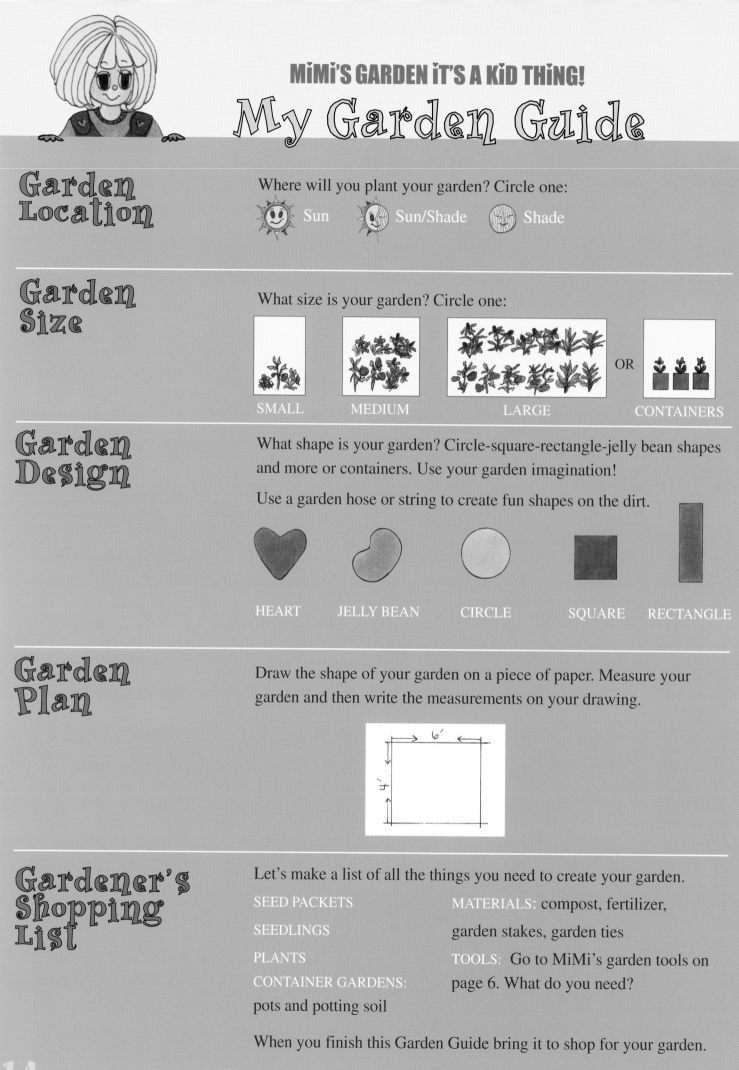

Garden Location

Where will you plant your garden? Circle one:

☀ Sun   ☁ Sun/Shade   ▦ Shade

Garden Size

What size is your garden? Circle one:

SMALL   MEDIUM   LARGE   OR   CONTAINERS

Garden Design

What shape is your garden? Circle-square-rectangle-jelly bean shapes and more or containers. Use your garden imagination!

Use a garden hose or string to create fun shapes on the dirt.

HEART   JELLY BEAN   CIRCLE   SQUARE   RECTANGLE

Garden Plan

Draw the shape of your garden on a piece of paper. Measure your garden and then write the measurements on your drawing.

Gardener's Shopping List

Let's make a list of all the things you need to create your garden.

SEED PACKETS

SEEDLINGS

PLANTS

CONTAINER GARDENS:
pots and potting soil

MATERIALS: compost, fertilizer, garden stakes, garden ties

TOOLS: Go to MiMi's garden tools on page 6. What do you need?

When you finish this Garden Guide bring it to shop for your garden.

Garden Symbols

Time To Plant

After danger of visits from Jack Frost

After leaves fall from the trees

Location

Full Sun

Sun/Shade

Shade

Watering

This plant likes the soil to be on the dry side between waterings.

This plant likes the soil to be slightly moist and to dry out a little bit between waterings.

This plant likes the soil to be moist to the touch. Don't let this plant droop from lack of water!

Feeding

Feed your plant once a week.

Feed your plant every two weeks.

Feed your plant once a month.

Feed according to special instructions.

Care

This plant loves a small amount of care.

This plant loves a medium amount of care.

This plant loves a large amount of care.

Turn the pages to discover great plants to grow!

Black-Eyed Susan

Rootball

1/2 soil and 1/2 compost
mixed together

BLACK-EYED SUSAN is nicknamed marmalade daisy. Thor's nickname is T and Maggie's is Miss Mags. Oskadis' nickname is Osk because it's easier to say. My nickname is Mim. Do you have a nickname that you like your garden friends to call you?

We dig our holes twice as wide and twice as deep as the BLACK-EYED SUSAN's rootball. This is the way we plant all of our flowers and vegetables. We give our plants special treatment to show them we care in MiMi's GARDEN.

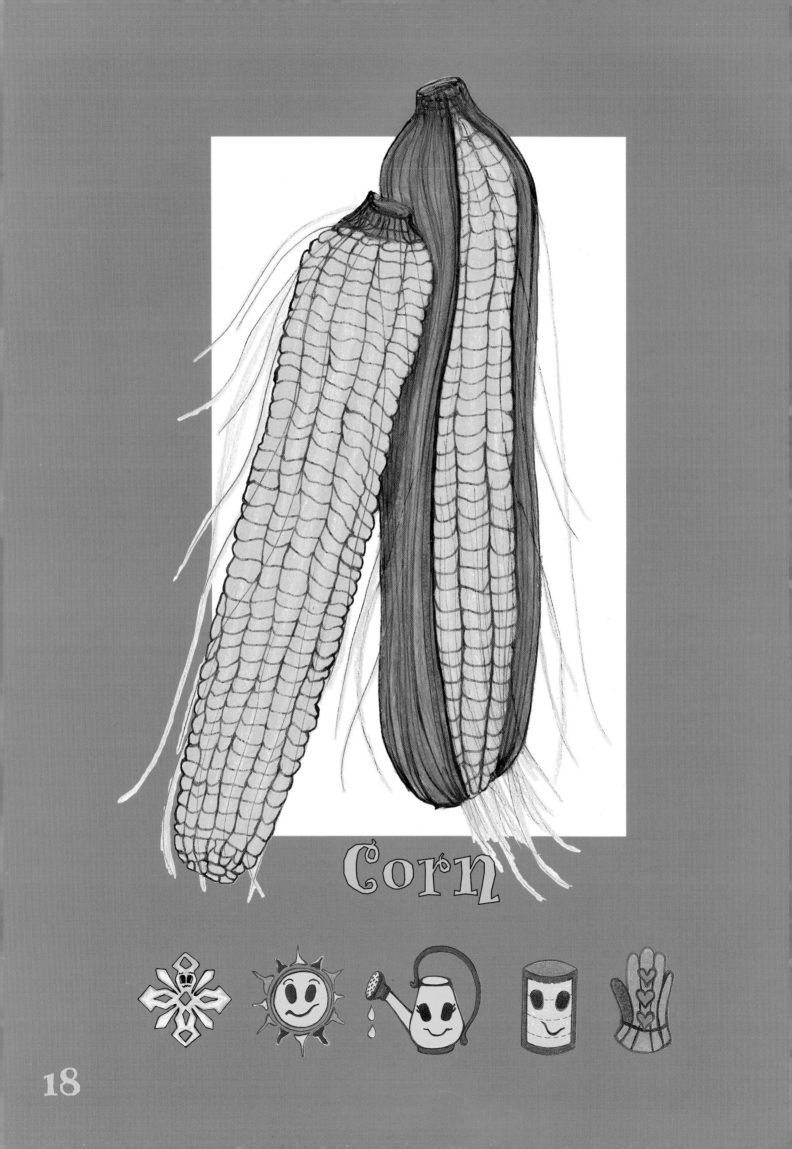

Corn

CORN patches are fun to grow. The wild birds love to eat our CORN. Mo, Rosa, Maggie and I built this great scarecrow and we named him Bob. Our scarecrow Bob was fun to make! He scares the wild birds away because we like to eat our CORN too! We had extra hay to dress ourselves up to look like Bob in our CORN patch. Which scarecrow is your favorite in MiMi's GARDEN?

Cosmos

COSMOS are very easy to start from seeds. They like soil that dries a little between waterings. COSMOS make pretty bouquets to share with our garden friends. They grow fast and come in several different colors! Look how tall our COSMOS have grown in MiMi'S GARDEN. We can play hide-n-seek! Can you help us find Maggie in our patch of COSMOS?

Impatiens

IMPATIENS come in lots of pretty colors. We planted our IMPATIENS in a wire basket filled with moss. We can move our basket of IMPATIENS anywhere in MiMi'S GARDEN. Mo and I are hanging our basket of IMPATIENS on a shepherd's hook for everyone to see. Our rose-colored IMPATIENS have grown so much they almost hide the basket. Can you see the wire basket?

Lemon Cucumber

24

LEMON CUCUMBER is a uniquely shaped cucumber. We plant seedlings 4 to 5 inches apart below our trellis. It is easier to harvest LEMON CUCUMBERS on a trellis. Rosa and I love to pick LEMON CUCUMBERS to share with our garden friends. My mom makes delicious LEMON CUCUMBER salads with tomatoes and Italian salad dressing. It tastes yummy! Maggie would you like to taste some?

Love-in-the-Mist

LOVE-IN-THE-MIST has delicate flowers that turn into fun seedpods. When the flowers dry up, the seeds in their pods can shake, rattle and roll. We can make great music from our garden! Today even though it's raining, we are making pretty LOVE-IN-THE-MIST bouquets to share from MiMi's GARDEN. Quick Thor, get under our big garden umbrella! Rain or shine, we garden all the time. Do you like to garden on a rainy day?

27

Peas

PEAS are my favorite vegetable. I love to pop fresh PEAS from the garden right out of their shell and into my mouth! They are tender and sweet. I think PEAS taste like candy. Mo says I can have his share of PEAS. Do you like to eat fresh PEAS from the garden? We are sowing a long row of PEAS in MiMi'S GARDEN. Make sure you space your PEA seeds with room to grow. We like to use a ruler for proper spacing. We can hardly wait for our PEAS to pop up!

Potatoes

POTATOES can grow in hay-covered soil! Would you like to plant POTATOES this way in your garden? Mo and I borrowed some hay from Oskadis for our POTATO patch. First, we placed the hay over the soil. Next, Mo nestles the POTATO down into the hay. Then, I cover the POTATO with big handfuls of hay. When the POTATOES sprout add more hay on top. You can plant them under the soil, too. Teamwork always makes MiMi's GARDEN grow!

Pumpkin

PUMPKINS always have a space in our garden. PUMPKIN plants can take up a lot of room in your garden. Their vines grow very big. PUMPKIN plants have big pretty flowers that turn into PUMPKINS. We scratch our names into our PUMPKINS when they are little and watch our names grow with our PUMPKINS. Who do you think should win the great PUMPKIN contest in MiMi'S GARDEN? We know who has Thor's vote!

Snapdragons

SNAPDRAGONS come in soft pastels and lots of pretty bright colors. They have beautiful flower spikes with lots of small flowers. SNAPDRAGONS have a hidden secret in MiMi'S GARDEN. They make great garden puppets! All you have to do is squeeze the sides of the little flower to make them talk. Mo and I love to share our SNAPDRAGON secrets. Maggie can hear our SNAPDRAGON secrets, too. What do you like to have your SNAPDRAGONS say to your garden friends?

Sunflower

SUNFLOWERS happily turn their faces to the sun in MiMi'S GARDEN. Our
SUNFLOWERS have large sunny faces. Every plant in our SUNFLOWER patch
has grown taller than us! MO and I cut several SUNFLOWERS with long stems
and let them dry out. We like to hang the SUNFLOWERS on the porch for instant
birdfeeders. Mo put one on his grandma's porch so she can watch the wild birds.
Would you like to feed the wild birds?

Tomatoes

Plant deep enough to cover most of the stem below the bottom leaves

Newspaper Collars

TOMATO plants need extra care. We plant them deep in the ground. Mo and I planted our TOMATOES with collars this year. My grandpa thinks collars are the best protection for TOMATOES! They are made from newspaper and will keep the bad bugs away. Our sturdy trellis keeps our TOMATOES off of the ground. We like to eat TOMATOES fresh and warm off the vines in our garden. Can you almost taste our juicy ripe TOMATOES?

Tulips

Read feeding instructions on the bag and then place food underneath the bulb when planting.

TULIPS are great for planting in containers and in the garden. TULIPS come in lots of different shapes, sizes and colors. Mo and I use organic soil for our TULIP bulbs. Our TULIPS pop up and it's not just luck! We always remember to plant TULIP bulbs with their pointy ends up. I like to water them with my favorite watering can. Maggie has her eye on our flower bowls. Sometimes she digs up things we plant. Maybe Maggie thinks she is helping! Do you have a dog that likes to help you dig in your garden?

Zinnias

ZINNIAS come in lots of fun colors. We lightly raked the soil before Mo, Rosa and I tossed ZINNIA seeds all around the garden. They popped up everywhere with very little care. Neighbors and friends love to buy our ZINNIAS. We save all our money for new plants, seeds and projects in MiMi'S GARDEN. Who didn't follow MiMi to the ZINNIA patch? You guessed it. Maggie was off digging in our flower bowls!

Dear America's Royal Gardener,
Our friend MiMi is a great gardener. She has taught us that gardening takes teamwork. Doing things together in the garden is fun and gets the job done faster!

We have learned to grow things from seeds. It takes patience. MiMi showed us how to harvest from MiMi's garden. It is fun to share what we have grown. But best of all MiMi has taught us in MiMi's garden it's a kid thing! Please pick our garden friend MiMi as the royal gardener this week.

Your garden friends,

Mo Rosa

...s royal gardener, MiMi
...is a great gardener.
...s many things in
...e has taught us
...s teamwork.
...n the garden is
...e faster!
...hings from
...i showed
...mimi's
...at we
...has
...kid

Guess what happened today? My garden friends sent this letter to our local newspaper. They were filled with pride as they opened the paper to our garden section and said, "Here read this!" Mo and Rosa had nominated me for the Royal Gardener of the week! My garden dream has come true!